This book belongs to:

....

....

....

FIRST EDITION

www.christianravello.com

ISBN: 978-0-6454439-0-5

This book is dedicated
to all the beautiful mothers in the world.
Thank you for your love, kindness and warmth.

Author books:

 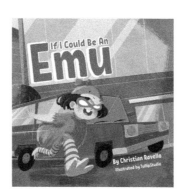 

Gemma Giraffe's SORE NECK

By Christian Ravello

Illustrated by Sasha Staneva

It happened in the early morning
as I lay in bed—
all sore and kind of wobbly
from my neck up to my head.

And once or twice, I tried to yawn
to help it go away.
But with my mouth wide open,
I just didn't feel okay.

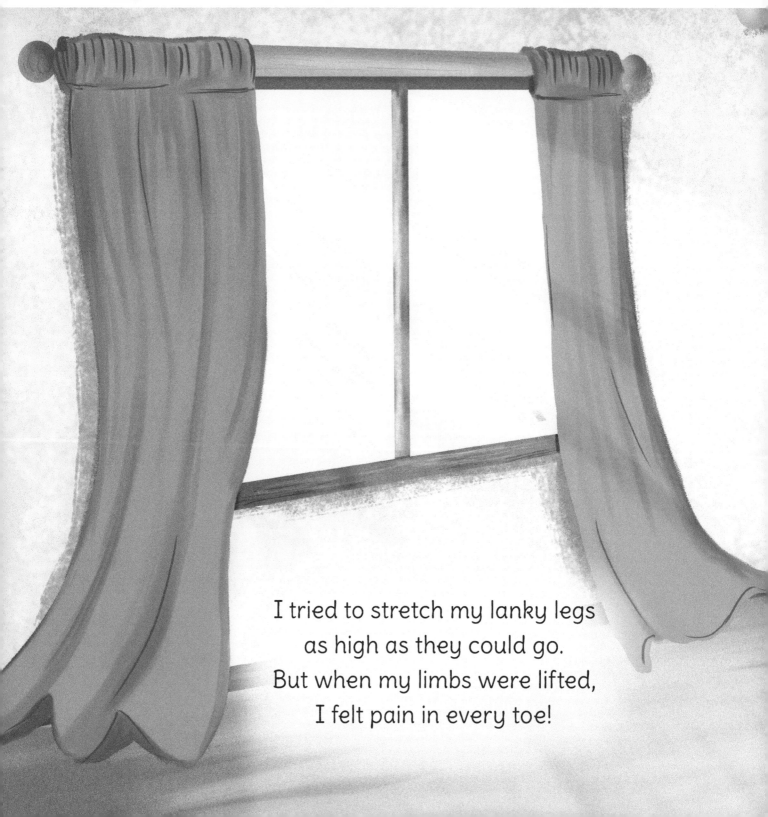

I tried to stretch my lanky legs
as high as they could go.
But when my limbs were lifted,
I felt pain in every toe!

I tried to call my mother
so she'd tell me what was wrong.
In vain, my voice called out to her
without a sound or song.

But somehow—just like magic —
she could hear my silent plea.
The bedroom door swung open
as she hurried in to see . . .

With tender loving kindness,
she provided one big hug.
But every time that I looked up,
my neck began to tug.

I told her that my neck hurt
and my throat felt really lumpy.
I stretched and yawned and winced.
I'd never felt so sad and grumpy!

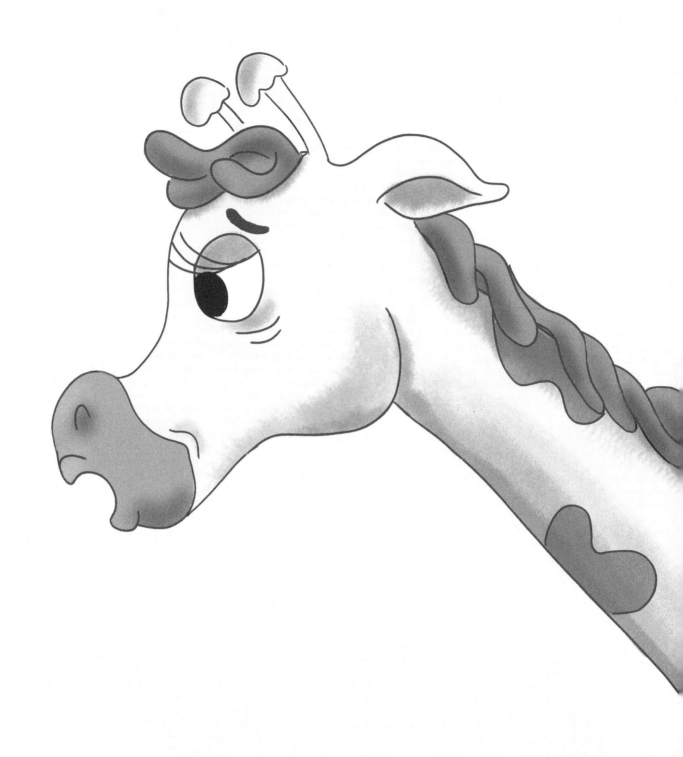

She brought me milk and carrots.
Then, she wiped my tears away—
played dress-up, read me storybooks
and sat with me all day.

From all our smiles and laughter,
soon, my neck began to mend.
It started feeling soft and loose;
I saw that it could bend.

The stars that night were shining bright
when I got back to bed.
A kiss goodnight from Mummy
let me dream and rest my head.

THE
END

Lightning Source UK Ltd.
Milton Keynes UK
UKHW050015210622
404695UK00002B/43

9 780645 443905